Complete Poetry of An Addict

Complete Edition

Brett C. Persson

Complete Poetry of an Addict

Cover art and Illustrations by S.C. Persson

Paperback ISBN:
978-1-964793-91-7

Nudous Publishing, LLC

This is a work of fiction. Names, places, characters, and events are either the product of the author's imagination or are used fictitiously, and any resemblance to any persons, living or dead, businesses, establishments, or locations is entirely coincidental.

This book is dedicated to my wife Kim, my parents Raymond and Beverly and my brother Jeff, my three daughters, Kinsey, Sara, and Baylie, and finally, to my granddaughter Emma.

12/13/19

The following collection consists of over 250 poems that I have written. Some I have written while under the influence of drugs and alcohol, and some have been written since I became drug-free. The oldest poem in this collection is from 1987 when I was fourteen years old.

The first portion of the book contains all my poems and are basic in their style and form. The ideas in most of them are strong, if not good, though in others I know they have no real point. Some will have meaning for a select few and those people will know who they are. The second portion of the book is all the Haiku I have written.

I don't want to be, or claim to be, a great poet. I am just an addict who threw some ideas into words that rhymed. This, I know, is no great feat. However, I was hoping it would help me see things differently, and in some cases, it did.

I named this collection 'Complete Poetry of an Addict' because that is what I am: an addict. I have tried many drugs and I never tried one I didn't like. I have done many things I am not proud of, but

I regret very few. Life is too short to live with regrets. If I focused on the things, I have done wrong over the years I would not be able to maintain my recovery.

My sobriety is the most important thing in my life, even more than my family in ways. If I was unable to maintain my sobriety my family would not be around. By putting my sobriety first, I am also putting my family first. The poems that follow are listed randomly. I wish I had a chronological order to them for my own curiosity if nothing else, but there is no way to reconstruct that information.

I don't know what will come tomorrow I just know for today I will remain sober and drug-free, I'll worry about tomorrow when it comes.

Brett C. Persson

Poem 1

It's the Dawn of a New Day
My Demons Now at Bay

My Head Now Clear
But Still Full of Fear

I Don't Know What's to Come
But I Know Where I Come From

Clear of The Dope
Now Full of Hope

Ready to Fight
To Face the Light

Poem 2

Walking in the Park
Strolling in the Dark

What a Wonderful Night
Stars So Bright

Feeling the Gentle Air
We Are a Pair

As We Round the Block
Our Fingers Interlock

She Completes My Life
She Is My Wife

I Am Sure You See
We Will Always Be

Poem 3

See Him Fall
Here Him Call

See the Gun
Watch Him Run

To Get Away
To Live Another Day

See the Hammer Hit
Might as Well Quit

Here the Shot
It's So Hot

Blood Begins to Flow
Nowhere to Go

Poem 4

In My Grave
For Being Brave

Shot in The Chest
While Doing My Best

My Heart Begins to Race
As I Look at His Face

Poem 5

My Future Is Looking Very Bleak
A Shotgun to My Cheek

Sweat Drips from My Balls
As the Hammer Falls

Know Filled with Led
My Blood Runs Red

Over My Lost Love Beth
I Cause My Own Death

Poem 6

Here at the Game
Never the Same

Throw the Ball Around
Tackle to the Ground

Make A Score
Never A Bore

Reach the End Zone
Set the Games Tone

Go All the Way
Make Them Pay

Poem 7

Fall in Love with A Girl
Pretty as A Pearl

It Was Great at First
But the Bubble Burst

She Ripped Out My Heart
When She Said We Had to Part?

Now I Know
Women Are Your Foe

She Was Everything to Me
Now She's Free

I Miss Her Still
And I Guess I Always Will

I Paid the Toll
She Took My Soul

Without Love, Life Is Dead

Poem 8

Give A Cheer
Drink A Beer

Begin to Smoke
Tell A Joke

Drink Some Wine
You're Feeling Fine

Beginning to Lean
From Too Much Jim Bean

Do Some Pot
Your Minds Beginning to Rot

Find A Mate
It's Getting Late

Got to Go
Alcohol Is My Foe

Busted For DUI
For Drinking Too Much Rye

Poem 9

Drink at A Bar
Drive Your Car

Smoke A Bowl
Hit A Pole

Cannot Walk
Cannot Talk

Drunk Behind the Wheel
You Cannot Feel

Poem 10

There Is No Cell
Straight to Hell

You Wanted Fame
But You Lost the Game

Your Soul Is Gone
What Went Wrong

Poem 11

The American Flag
Nothing More Than A Rag

We Lost Our Pride
To the Other Side

We Went to Prison
As Their Flag Was Risen

We Did Not Care
So, In Came the Bear

Nothing to Fight For
The Eagle Is No More

Poem 12

Got My First Chip
Was Going to Dip

Read from The Book
It Was Worth A Look

It Was Big and Blue
But It Rang True

Words from The Wise
To Avoid My Demise

I Had Reach My End
Light Around the Bend

Poem 13

I Sit in My Chair
I Receive A Glare

I See Her Pain
Nothing to Gain

I See Her Tears
So Many Fears

They Put on My Hood
I've Done No Good

Now I'm Frightened
As the Straps Are Tightened

The Lights Dim
Future's Grim

Poem 14

I Had the Gun
Oh, What Fun

Shot Her Dead
In His Bed

I Know What's Right
What A Sight

See Her Bleed
That's What I Need

Vengeance Is Done
I Had the Gun

Poem 15

I Hear Her Lies
I See Her Die

She Caused Me Pain
So Much to Gain

I Feel Her Heart
Now We Part

What A Shame
Death Is My Game

Poem 16

I Hit It Hard
The Crystal Shard

It Begins to Smoke
A Take a Toke

I Feel It Fast
Forget the Past

Release a Big Sigh
Soaring So High

The Pipe Falls from My Hand
Life is so Grand

So Much More Drive
Feeling So Alive

Poem 17

She Sees My Grin
She Prepares for My Sin

She Feels the Blade
She Becomes Afraid

She Tastes My Breath
She Nears Death

She Smells My Hate
She Meets Her Fate

Poem 18

Cut Down to Size
For All of Her Lies

Shot in The Back
Life She Now Lacks

Kick Her Chest
Cut Her Breast

Twist Her Neck
Now Who's the Wreck

Feel Her Life Ebb Away
Toss Her Body in The Bay

Poem 19

Standing High
Ready to Fly

Looking Down
Over the Town

Yes or No
Should I Go

What Life Do I Lead
How Much Will I Bleed

People Yelling
How Compelling

Society Is Sick
They Get A Kick

Watch Me Fly
Here Me Die

Poem 20

Slit Your Wrist
Clench Your Fist

See It Run
Now There Is None

No Pain to Feel
Life No Longer Real

Poem 21

Pull A Gun
Let's Have Fun

Shoot Him Down
Watch Her Frown

Take His Money
Rape His Honey

Poem 22

Take His Life
With Your Knife

Stab the Bastard Dead
All You See Is Red

He Killed Your Kid
That's What He Did

Poem 23

Starting to Hunt
For That Cunt

She Laughed at Me
Watch Her Pee

As I Snap Her Neck
Oh, What the Heck

I Guess to Violent
Now She Is Silent

Poem 24

I Hear the War
Killing the Poor

I Hear the Shots
Killing the Tots

I Hear the Plane
So Much Pain

I Hear Them Cry
So, Say Goodbye

Poem 25

Begin to Puke
You Shot the Nuke

Only Choice, So True
It Was Them Not You

No Winners
All Sinners

See the Light
With All It's Might

Poem 26

Tip the Drink Back
Start to Hack

Feel It Burn
Quench That Urn

Go to A Rave
You Are A Slave

On Life's Brink
Because What You Drink

Poem 27

Here Another Day
What Can I Say

Sentenced to Life
Lost My Wife

The Cell Closed
My Life Hosed

Getting Out to Late
She Won't Wait

Except for the Guy with The Bone
I Am All Alone

Poem 28

I Feel a Chill
It Is There Still

Feel Something Wrong
For So Long

Don't Want to Make A Noise
Or Lose My Poise

Maybe It Will Go Away
And No Longer Stay

I Can Feel Him Here
God Take My Fear

Who Is This Stranger
That Puts Me in Danger

He is Not Natural
He Is Pastural

Poem 29

Feel the Sun
Have Some Fun

Play Some Ball
It's Almost Fall

Forget the Frill
Light the Grill

Eat Some Food
Some Get Rude

Tell Them to Stop
He Gets the Drop

You Lay on The Floor
Look at The Gore

Your Life Leaks Out
You Have No Doubt

Filled with Fear
Cause Death Is Near

Poem 30

Look at This Place
Too Much Focus on Race

See What Is Inside
You Don't Have to Hide

Be What You Will
You Don't Have to Kill

Color Is Skin Deep
Be Careful What You Reap

So Be Ever So Kind
Cause Death Is Blind

Poem 31

You Go to The Store
You Know What For

You Pull Your Gun
People Begin to Run

Take A Man's Honey
Ask for The Money

Put the Gun to Her Head
They Were Just Wed

Grab the Cash
Make A Dash

Shoot the Groom
Certain Doom

Bring Her Along
Soon She'll Be Gone

Made A Quick Fifty
Isn't That Nifty

Poem 32

Cuffed Behind Your Back
Because You're Black

Beaten with A Stick
By Some Private Dick

Slammed in To the Car
They're Going to Far

Forced to Tell A Lie
Now You'll Fry

Because Of You Skin
You Can't Win

Poem 33

I Stumble and Fall
Trapped in a Wall

My Life Seeps Away
Left Here to Decay

No One Heard a Sound
I Will Not Be Found

Poem 34

You Start to Get A Doubt
As the Lights Go Out

You Pull Out the Mac
To Kill A Pack

Car Slows Down
People Start to Frown

Going for Their Guns
And Pushing Down Their Huns

They're Too Late
You Have Sealed Their Fate

You Pull the Trigger
Who Would Have Figured

Killed Them All
You Will Take the Fall

For Killing Such A Mass
They'll Give You the Gas

Poem 35

Hit Him with The Car
You Went Too Far

Had too Much Beer
To Hide Your Fear

Know You Have Killed
It's What You Willed

Poem 36

Cut the Line
You're Feeling Fine

Feel It Burn
You'll Never Learn

Nose Begins to Bleed
You're Mind Feeing

Poem 37

It Burns Going In
I Know It's a Sin

It Feels So Right
My Throat so Tight

I Can't Go Without
There is No Doubt

It's Easy to Start
So Hard to Part

I Know I'm Sick
But It's a Trick

We Once Fought
But It Bends My Thought

I Don't Resist Much
I've Lost Touch

Poem 38

Mind Begins to Wonder
As You Begin to Ponder

What Happened to My Life
When I Lost My Wife

Killed by A Gun
Before the Rise of The Sun

Penetrated by A Thug
On Your Heart It Does Tug

Poem 39

The Echoes of Life
Show So Much Strife

Fueled by Hate
I Killed Kate

She Was My Boss
No Big Loss

Who Will Know
How I Killed Her So

Poem 40

Starting to Roll
Drugs Taking Its Toll

Hearing A Jingle
Beginning to Tingle

Jaw Clenched Tight
Everything Seems Right

Sweat Lining My Brow
Hitting Hard Now

Taking Leaps and Bounds
World Swirling Around

Poem 41

Skidding on The Ice
Praying the Price

Losing Control
Heading for The Pole

Hitting It Hard
Draw the Death Card

Glass in Your Face
As You Brace

Bones Shatter Apart
Your Body They Soon Cart

No Chance to Live
Nothing More to Give

Your Blood Runs Out
You Have No Doubts

Life Ebbing Away
Now Your Turn to Pay

Heart Stops to Beat
Dead in Your Car Seat

Poem 42

I Smoke My Grass
So, Kiss My Ass

I'm Your Cross-To Bear
You Say You Care

You Throw A Fit
What Bullshit

Drugs Are Grand
You Don't Understand

Poem 43

I Hear the Sound
Feelings Abound

We Begin to Dance
Caught in Your Trance

Feeling So Fine
Now That You're Mine

You Have My Hart
Love Off the Chart

Hold Me Tight
You Are My Light

Poem 44

Drugs in My Veins
Heading Down the Lanes

Everything Is Fast
No Looking to The Past

In Paradise Now
I Know How

Shooting It In
I Know I'll Win

I Love My Stuff
If You Don't Like It Tuff

Poem 45

Driving My Car
To the Bar

To Get My Fix
From My Mix

Drink It Down
Erase My Frown

I Get into A Rant
Life It Does Grant

Poem 46

Hard to Say What I Feel
Trying to Keep It Real

You Don't Want to Hear
About My Fear

You Want a Perfect Kid
Well You Lost That Bid

Need Help on The Double
I Am in Trouble

I Have Losing Who I Am
My Soul on the Lam

My End I Think Is Not Far
My Life Not on Par

Wish I Could Have Made You Happy
You and Pappy

It is Time for Me to Go
I Hope It Isn't Slow

Poem 47

A Sense of Clarity
Which Is A Rarity

Higher Then A Kite
Full of Might

Rolling Opens the Mind
Feeling So Kind

Knowing It All
Drugs I Hear Call

Chew Them Up
Feeling Like A Pup

What Joys It Brings
Thinking I Have Wings

Poem 48

It's Starting to Flow
There Is No Low

Mind Begins to Race
Let Me Make My Case

Drugs Open the Mind
I Think You Will Find

Feeling So Grand
As You Listen to The Band

Feeling So Strong
Nothing Is Wrong

Come on In
And Watch Me Grin

Poem 49

Grabbing the Gun
Having Some Fun

One Bullet In
Who Will Win

Spin the Wheel
What to Feel

Pull the Trigger
Go Figure

Taunting Death
Maybe Your Last Breath

Poem 50

Trapped in My Cell
After I Fell

Silenced in My Guilt
For This Life I Built

Used to Be Hot
But Here I Will Rot

Poem 51

I Hear Her Cry
My Turn to Die

Leaving Her Behind
Peace I Hope She Will Find

Taken to Early
Away from My Girly

Now She Is Alone
How Much She Has Grown

Stronger Then When We Met
Stronger She Will Get

She Will Proceed Through Life
As A Widowed Wife

Poem 52

Getting Away from It All
Having A Ball

Head in The Sky
From Getting So High

At Peace with It for Now
I Am Not Sure How

Got to Keep It Real
Got TO Remember to Feel

Let the Emotions Out
Without A Doubt

Poem 53

Their Eyes Tear My Up
Like a Lost Pup

I Feel Them Cutting Me
Just Want to Be Free

I Am Bleeding
They Are Feeding

They Are Taking Who I Am
Life Such a Sham

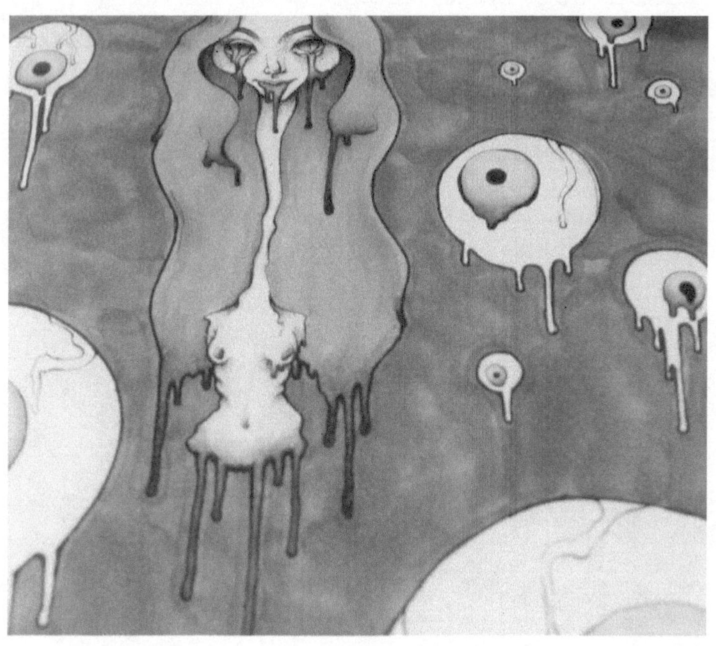

Poem 54

Sunday Morning, I Awake
Give Me A Break

My Body Is Sore
Moving Is A Chore

Memories of Past Night
Somewhat of A Fright

Visions of My Life
Cause So Much Self Strife

Must Get Some More
Keep the Pain Off of The Shore

The Only Way to Function
During A Life Junction

Lost in A Bar
Feel Like A Shooting Star

Soon to Burn Out
Life Is What I Doubt

Stuck in A Bottle
Life Full Throttle

Poem 55

Wishing I Was Done
But It Is Too Much Fun

Wishing I Was Clean
But I Like Being Mean

Wishing I Was Fine
But on Drugs I Dine

Wishing for Clarity
But I Instead I Look for Charity

Wishing I Had A Friend
But Myself I Only Tend

Wishing I Had Listened to Dad
But I Guess I Was too Bad

Wishing I Knew It All
But Instead I Fall

Wishing for Love
But My Life Fits Like A Glove

Wishing for Hope
But Instead I Use Dope

Wishing I Had Some Dreams
But I Don't It Seems

Wishing to Be Free
But to Wrapped Up in Me

Wishing to Calm Down
But I’m A Fucking Clown

Wishing I Hadn’t Failed
But Life I Bailed

Wishing I Had Stayed Straight
But I Took the Bait

Wishing to Turn It Around
But the Drugs Keep Me Sound

Wishing I Was Dead
But to The Drugs I Am Wed

Wishing to Lose This Curse
But I Keep the Drugs to Nurse

Wishing to Stop Getting High
But I Never Try

Wishing I Had Made Them Proud
But My Shame Is My Shroud

Wishing for Relief
But I Have No Belief

Wishing I Was More
But I Still Look to Score

Wishing I Was Rich
But I Believe My Own Pitch

Wishing I Had A Wife
But I Lost Out in Life

Wishing I Could Think on My Own
But I Am So Prone

Wishing God to Save My Heart
But I Thing We Grew Apart

Wishing I Would Stop and Think
But My Life Is on The Brink

Wishing to Be Heard
But How Absurd

Wishing to Be Cured
But I am Still Lured

Wishing I Could See the Light
But My Addiction Wins the Fight

Wishing to Be with A Lover
But My Feelings I Cover

Wishing to Be Better
But I Try to Be A Trend Setter

Wishing to Be Like You
But I Loose at Whatever I DO

Wishing to Be Without A High
But to Myself I Lie

Wishing to Go Places
But I Can't See Their Faces

Wishing I Could Remember
But My Mind Is A Dying Ember

Wishing I Was Dry
But in The End, I Will Die

Wishing I Was Right
But Instead I Live in Fright

Wishing I Could Live in The Past
But I Know I will Finish Last

Wishing to Be Like My Brother
But I Am Too Much Like My Mother

Wishing She Had Been Cleaner
But She Could Have Been Meaner

Wishing to Be the Best
But I Will Die Like the Rest

Wishing Love, I Could Find
But My Soul Is in A Bind

Wishing I Was Profound
But the Drugs I Pound

Wishing I Could Study
But Drugs Are My Buddy

Wishing to Be More Bold
But My Soul I Have Sold

Wishing to Be A Better Man
But the Shit Hits the Fan

Wishing to Feel Something Grand
But on My Feet, I Never Land

Wishing to Soar Like A Bird
But I Followed the Wrong Herd

Wishing to Feel Something Inside
But the Joy of Drugs Is What I Ride

Wishing to Get A Helping Hand
But I Listen to The Drug Band

Wishing I Was God
But Instead I Shoot My Wad

Wishing I Was King
But I Loose in The Ring

Wishing for Salvation
But I Sealed My Damnation

Wishing for Some Support
But My Family I Deport

Wishing for More Time
But I Am Such A Slime

Wishing It Was Just Glee
But Others I See

Wishing for One Great Day
But I Still Pay

Wishing I Wasn't Broke
But I Still Take A Toke

Wishing I Was A Better Child
But I Was to Wild

Wishing to Eat
But I Am to Beat

Wishing to Make A Stand
But I Sink in The Sand

Wishing to Grow
But I Can't Seem to Show

Wishing I Got More Puss
But I Around Women I Am A Wuss

Wishing to Find A Mate
But I'm Always Out Late

Wishing to Feel Some Joy
But I treat People Like A Toy

Wishing to Be Taught
But Instead I Was Caught

Wishing to Lead
But Hung Up on Speed

Wishing to Be on Top
But Busted by A Cop

Wishing I Was Rolling
But the Cops Are Strolling

Wishing I Was A Blast
But I Have No Sails on My Mast

Wishing to Remember Women I Met
But I Lost That Bet

Wishing I Knew My Lovers Name
But She Couldn't Do the Same

Wishing to Hear Her Call
But I Hit A Wall

Wishing to Feel Her Touch
But I Abused Her to Much

Wishing I Had the Balls to Jump
But in My Throat, There Is A Lump

Wishing to Not Be So Lean
But I Am Drug Fein

Wishing to Meet My Maker
But I Am A Taker

Wishing to Get My Fill
But I Can't Kill

Wishing to Rob A Bank
But I Don't Rank

Wishing to See the Sun
But I'm Was Always on The Run

Wishing to Be Asleep
But I'm In to Deep

Wishing to Just Be
But Life Charges A Fee

Wishing to Be Less Cold
But I Am Growing Old

Wishing to Quite This Crap
But Drugs Are A Snap

Wishing to Feel Something
But I Only Feel Nothing

Wishing I Could Draw
But I Chose the Short Straw

Wishing I Had A Calling
But It Feels More Like A Mauling

Wishing I Could Walk the Line
But I Never Shine

Wishing to Sail A Boat
But All I Do Is Float

Wishing to Do the Most
But All I Do Coast

Wishing to Be Martyr
But with My Soul I Did Barter

Wishing I Could Write
But I Don't Have the Inner Sight

Wishing I Was Sailing
But I'm Always Wailing

Wishing for That Ultimate Feeling
But Always Left Reeling

Wishing for A Chick
But No Strength in My Prick

Wishing for A Nice Girl
But I'm Caught in A Whirl

Wishing for A Lot
But Mind Continues to Rot

Wishing for Some Meaning
But the Drugs Keep Me Leaning

Wishing I Had A Better Teacher
But I Don't Hear the Preacher

Wishing to Be Understood
But I Know No One Could

Wishing I Had Made A Difference
But I Give No Reverence

Wishing I Was Not A Rat
But I'm A Door Mat

Wishing I Was Told
But They Always Fold

Wishing I Was on A Retreat
But the World Keeps Me Beat

Wishing I Was Not the Black Sheep
But That Is A Leap

Wishing A Could Cut the Hook
But Drugs Read Me Like A Book

Wishing I Could Get Laid
But Lately I Am to Afraid

Wishing the Paranoia Would Stop
But I Still Hear My Ears Pop

Wishing I Wasn't So Scarred
But No One Cared

Wishing I Wasn't in Jail
But No One Posted My Bail

Wishing I Was on The Ocean Floor
But I Can Take More

Wishing to Be Fair
But I Don't Dare

Wishing I Had Learned
But I Still Get Burned

Wishing My Brother Was Well
But He Hears the Death Bell

Wishing I Was One with Him
But I Think He Is A Whim

Wishing It Was True
But All I Feel Is Blue

Wishing Life, I Had Mastered
But I Am Bastard

Wishing on My Four-Leaf Clover
But the Game Is Over

Wishing It Wasn't My Fault
But in My Wound People Place Salt

Wishing the Accident Had Killed
But I Wasn't the One Chilled

Wishing for Some Free Food
But I Am to Rude

Wishing for A Place to Lay
But They Will Not Let Me Stay

Wishing I Was Chosen
But I Got Such A Hosen

Wishing People Would Call Me Mister
But I Get No Respect from My Sister

Wishing I Could See My House
But I Was A Louse

Wishing I Had A Child
But Life Was Not That Mild

Wishing I Had Beer
But There Is Nothing to Cheer

Wishing I Was Far Away
But I Linger at Bay

Wishing I Could Still Bread
But I Can't Spread My Seed

Wishing I Could Pray
But All I Can Do Is Play

Poem 56

Waking Up on The Wrong Side
Her Eyes Open Wide

Slap the Bitch Around
Screaming Abound

She Pulls Out the Gun
No More Fun

She Pulls the Slide Back
For Your Attack

The Bullet Rips Threw Your Skin
There Are No Grins

You Fall Down Dead
Tears She Will Shed

Poem 57

Feeling the Pain of Being
Of the Things I am Seeing

How the World Has Changed
Gotten So Fucking Deranged

Brother Versus Brother
Everyone Killing Each Other

In the Name of a God
Or in a Jihad

Watch People Die
For No Reason Why

Struggles of the Modern Man
Just Because They Can

Poem 58

Stuck in Life
With My Wife

She is Stuck with Me
Neither of Us Free

We Both Like It This Way
Small Price to Pay

Stuck Like Glue
Love Like So Few

Poem 59

Shoot the Gun
Start to Run

Try to Get Away
It's Not A Game You Play

Shoot to Kill
Against Your Will

Go to Jail
No Posted Bail

Go to Trial
For Killing Kyle

You Don't Have A Dime
So, Serve Your Time

Justice Is Sold
Truth Never Told

Poem 60

Took Her Son
Gave Him A Gun

Sent Him to War
Hear Him Roar

He Became the Best
But Was Shot in The Chest

Died for What Was Right
Tried with All His Might

He Wanted to Be Back
In His Nice Little Shack

His Mothers Grief
Scatter His Ashes on The Reef

Poem 61

Wasted on Meth
Fearing No Death

Enjoying the High
Using It to Get By

Letting You Soul Soar
That's What It Is For

Feeling at Ease
It Likes to Please

Fills You with Power
As High as A Tower

Hearing in Tune
Starring at The Moon

Wondering What Is Out There
Ferocious as A Bear

Sometimes You Rage
Trapped in A Cage

Losing All Control
Keeping Up with Parole

Watching Out for The Cops
Fuck All the Whops

Enjoying the Thrills
Shaking the Chills

Lost in Your Own Mind
Nothing in There to Find

Poem 62

Open the Door
Slide on The Floor

Tip the Bottle Back
Sobriety You Soon Lack

Feeling It Burn
Feeling the Mind Turn

To A Place More Known
A Place Well Flown

Vision Begins to Blur
You Are Quite Sure

You Don't Care
Because You Are There

You Are in That Place
Now at Your Pace

Starting to Blackout
There Is No Doubt

Forget the Bash
Soon to Crash

Wake Up the Next Day
In Your Own Puke You Lay

Soon You Will Start the Ritual
Because You Are Habitual

Can’t Stay Straight
The Bottle Is You Fate

Poem 63

Hit the Crack Pipe
Smelling Kind of Ripe

Sitting in A Gutter
Sucking on Addictions Utter

Bring It on In
All of Satan's Sin

Stealing Money
Life Not Funny

Sitting in Your Piss
Begging from Younger Sis

Mugging the Old
Always So Cold

For A Five-Minute High
Your Soul Will Die

Crack on Your Brain
A Life Filled of Pain

You Need A Shower
But You Have No Power

The Reaper Counts the Days
While You're in A Haze

His Sickle Is Near
You Have No Fear

Poem 64

I Got the Pills
For the Thrills

Crunch Them Well
Escape from My Hell

Drift Away from It All
Having A Ball

Away from The Burdens of Life
Forgetting About All the Strife

Lost in My Own Little Place
Forget About the Rat Race

Soaring to The Highest High
You Know Why

Reality Sucks Me Dry
That Is Why I Fly

I'll Set You Free
If You Come with Me

Poem 65

Watch Them Run
Behind the Setting Sun

Bullets Begin to Spray
Kill They May

Time for Them to Die
Drug Deal Gone A Rye

They Won't Cheat Me
You Will See

Poem 66

Feeling So Sad
Because I Was Bad

This Will Soon Pass
Playing in The Grass

I Try as I Might
But Can't Always Be Right

Poem 67

Did You Here It All
On That Call

She Is Out of Her Mind
You Will Find

Says It's My Kid
Fucked Her Once I Did

But That Don't Make It So
She Wants My Dough

Can't Be My Seed
Off Me She Will Feed

Fucking Whore
What She Is keeping It For

To Suck Me Dry
That's Why

Poem 68

Sweating in The Dark
Alone in The Park

Beginning to See
The Darkness in Me

Soul So Black
Compassion I Lack

Satan's Hardened My Heart
When God Made Us Part

I Lost My Life
When God Took My Wife

Now Nothing to Live For
I Have Nothing More

She Was the Best
Fuck the Rest

She Made Me Feel Alive
She Made Me Thrive

God Let Her Leave
I Still Can't Believe

Happy When We Wed
But Now I Feel Dead

I Miss Her So
Why Did She Go

I Want to End It All
I Want to Take A Fall

I'm Afraid to Die
I Got to Try

Got the Gun to My Head
My Blood I Will Shed

To Be with Her
But I Am Unsure

I Can't Go on Without Her Here
But I Am Filled with Fear

I Wish I Could Just Do It
Life I Want to Quit

Scared of What God Will Think
But I Am on The Brink

She Was My Best Friend
But Her I Could Not Defend

He Cut Her Down
All I Can Do Is Frown

He Got Away
He Will Never Pay

I Pull the Hammer Back
I Think I'm On the Right Track

I Will See Her Soon
I Die Under This Moon

Poem 69

Listen to Your Heart
It's Time to Part

She Betrayed Your Trust
Relationship A Bust

You Need to End It Now
Doesn't Matter How

She Says She Made A Mistake
She Is Such A Fake

Better Off Without Her
That Is for Sure

Poem 70

Sales Are Good
Better Then They Should

Hard Work Is the Key
Be All You Can Be

Making Good Money
To Support Your Honey

Your Life Is Grand
Money If You're Hand

Poem 71

The Love of Your Wife
Adds to Your Life

Hold Her Tight
She Feels So Right

Making Your Whole World Sound
Spreading the Kindness Around

God Led Me to Her
I Am Sure

She Accepted My Ring
That Was the Best Thing

She Is My Best Friend
Till the Bitter End

Poem 72

God Is in My Heart
His Love Off the Chart

Believing Makes A Life Worth Living
So, Keep on Giving

Be Sure to Help Others
Support Your Brothers

In Christ I Am Strong
I Feel Like A Belong

Sometimes It's Hard to Believe
That He Will Never Leave

He Will Always Help You Out
When You Are in Doubt

He Will Stand by Your Side
All Threw Life's Wild Ride

He Will Carry You
When You Think You Are Threw?

Shelter You in His Grace
Help You Win the Race

He Will Comfort Your Mind
When You Are in A Bind

His Love Has No End
Your Pain He Can Mend

Poem 73

Hanging on A Cross
Rocks They Will Toss

The Stick Him with A Spear
Because Of Their Fear

He Dies for Or Sin
He Will Always Win

He Preached His Ways
It Took Three Days

Rising from The Dead
Thorns on His Head

He Will Give You Salvation
Protect You from Damnation

Poem 74

The Grace of God Shines Down
Illuminates the Town

Spreading His Grace
All Over the Place

He Is Watching Us All
Making Sure We Don't Fall

Helping Us When We Need
By Word And Deed

Giving Us Hope
Helping Us to Cope

Placing His Arms Around Us
Without A Fuss

Everything Will Be Alright
When You See the Light

Poem 75

He Was A Teacher
And A Preacher

He Taught Us the Way
To Live Each Day

Wrote the Book
Hoping for Us to Look

He Wants Us to Be Kind
Even in A Bind

He Will Lift Your Heart
He Will Never Part

Even When We Are Wrong
We Still Belong

He Will Always Care for You
That's Nothing New

Trust in Him
It Isn't A Whim

Poem 76

Did You Ever Think
You Could Break the Link

He Will Always Watch Out for You
No Matter What You Do

Even If You Sway
Every Day

He Will Always Be There
For Your Grief to Share

Poem 77

Feeling Quite Right
With All You Might

From the Pills You Bite
You May Start A Fight

He May Be Black or White
Who Ever Is in Your Sight

From Any Height
You Have No Fright

You See No Light
No Matter How Bright

You Have So Much Spite
Mind in Flight

Fist Clenched Tight
In the Darkness of Night

Eyes Open Oh So Slight
You Are Not Polite

You Will Smite
Flying Higher Then A Kite

Poem 78

Covered Up in Bed
A Cold in Your Head

You Feel Like Shit
Your Fever Is Lit

Can't Shake This Feeling
Your Body Is Reeling

Wanting to Feel Better
Your Brow Grows Wetter

Hoping It Will Soon Be Gone
At Least By Dawn

You Hate Getting Sick
Feels Like You're Going to Kick

Poem 79

I Hear What Your Saying
But I Isn't Staying

Get It for Me
Or Let Me Be

How About Some of That Blow
Hurry I Need to Go

Just an Eight Ball
Before I Fall

I Need It Bad
Take It Back to My Pad

My Wife Is in Some Need
Her Nose to Feed

She Needs Her Coke
As Soon as She Awoke

She Is Waiting on It
Probably Throwing A Fit

As You Can Guess
She Is A Mess

Poem 80

I See the Car
Sitting Afar

Windows Tinted Dark
Next to The Park

Waiting for The Right Time
To Drop the Dime

Watching My Every Move
Getting into My Groove

Seeing What I Do
Oh, So True

For Some Fee
He Wants to Kill Me

Got in Someone's Way
Now I Have to Pay

I Could Try and Run
But I Know I'm Done

Soon He Will Win
And I'll Die for My Sin

Poem 81

Read My Lips
Feel My Hips

Turn Off the Light
Make It So Right

Make It Rough
I Am Tough

Passion Set A Fire
Like A Funeral Pire

Poem 82

I See A Waste Land
Nothing but Sand

Used to Be Lush
But Now There Is No Brush

All the Trees Are Gone
So Is the Lawn

Buildings Are No More
Devastated by Nuclear War

There Is No One Here
That Is Clear

Poem 83

I See My Shrink
I'm On the Brink

He Knows Me Well
I Know He Can Tell

Feeling So Sad
Never Glad

Always Thinking of The Worst
Never Putting Me First

Always Trying to Make Others Happy
While I Feel Crappy

He Seems to Help Me
This Much I See

Always Lends Me an Ear
When I Talk About My Fear

Poem 84

He Gets in His Car
He Will Drive Far

Going on Vacation
Across the Nation

Taking A Small Trip
To Places That Are Hip

Going to Meet
People to Greet

Nothing to Plan
Just the Car and The Man

Poem 85

I Bought You Candy
That Was Dandy

I Bought You Wine
So, We Could Dine

I Bought You A Charm
I Figured What's the Harm

I Bought You A Cat
But There She Sat

I Bought You Lunch
But I Had A Hunch

I Bought You A Car
But Not Up to Par

I Bought You A Ring
You Didn't Say A Thing

I Bought You So Much
But You No Longer Touch

I Bought You Gold
But You Were So Cold

I Bought You A Couch
You Said I'm A Slouch

I Bought Us A House
You Called Me A Louse

Poem 86

Hard to Feel My Feet
After My Drug Treat

Washed It Down with Wine
Feeling Oh So Fine

My Mind Floating Around
Love This Feeling I Found

Got to Do This Again Next Week
I'm Turning into A Freak

Wondering Why I Didn't Do It Before
There Is So Much More

Hope to Find This Place Again Soon
Eyes as Large as The Moon

Poem 87

Running Out of Time
Such A Crime

She Needs A Heart
So, She Won't Depart

Days Tick Away
Too Weak to Play

Can Hardly Walk
Hard Just to Talk

She Is My First Born
My Soul Is Torn

Poem 88

Along for The Ride
Eyes Open Wide

Swerving in His Lane
You Are Insane

To Ride with A Drunk
You're Such A Punk

Shouldn't Have Gotten In
Car in A Spin

Hitting A Tree
Nowhere to Flee

Through the Windshield
You Land in A Field

Laying in A Heap
Face Cut Deep

Bleeding into The Dirt
With Death You Do Flirt

The Reaper Draws Near
Filled with Fear

Your Mom Will Cry
When You Die

Peace Never Found
Cause You’re in The Ground

It Will Pain Her So
Should’ve Said No

Poem 89

Stalking Like A Cat
A Girl Name Pat

Want Her So Bad
It Makes Me Mad

Must Get to Her
That's for Sure

Take Her by Force
But Of Course

I Draw Near
She Turns in Fear

I Take Out My Knife
So, I Can Take Her Life

She Grabs for Her Gun
Now I Need to Run

She Shoots at Me
I Cannot Flee

I Hit the Floor
At Deaths Door

Couldn't Stop the Voices
I Made the Wrong Choices

A See the Cloaked Man Approach
I Will Ride His Coach

Off to The Other Side
I Shall Ride

Cause I Wasn't Right
I See No Light

Poem 90

See Mr. Dunn
Begin to Run

Chasing After Mr. Glass
He's After His Ass

He Is Now in Sight
Fighting for What Is Right

Must Stop Him Fast
Before Another Blast

Send Elijah To Jail
Dunn Must Not Fail

He Has Already Escaped Once
He Is No Dunce

Poem 91

In My Leather Chair
It Is Not Fair

My Chest Gets Tight
I Begin to Fight

Pain in My Arm
Major Cause for Alarm

Feeling Kind of Sick
Death I Can't Lick

My Heart in Arrest
Should've Had the Test

I Put It Off to Long
I Guess I Was Wrong

Dead at Thirty-Three
Just Remember Me

Poem 92

My Beeper Signals Me
Time to Collect My Fee

Got to Get My Cash
Just A Quick Dash

Selling Drugs Is My Game
Everyone Knows My Name

I Can Get It All
Big or Small

Whatever Your Need
I Can Surely Feed

I Am Large
And in Charge

I Am the Man to See
They Never Let Me Be

Always Working on A Deal
Cause Wounds Drugs Do Heal

Making Sure I Got Enough
It Is Sometimes Tough

But It Keeps Business Good
Go Somewhere Else They Could

Poem 93

Woke Up from a Daze
Everything Still in a Haze

It was Rough Night
No End in Sight

I Know I was Loud
I Ain't Proud

I Get Carried Away
Without Any Delay

Lose Control Fast
But What a Blast

Poem 94

A Love to Write
Sometimes I Bite

Wish I Was Something Great
Most of It I Hate

I Have the Will
But I Lack the Skill

Poem 95

School Would Have Been Smart
But from It I Did Depart

Could Have Learned More
Instead I Wanted to Score

Wanted to Get High
So, I Skated on By

Didn't Learn Shit
So Unemployed I Sit

Not Doing Anything Productive
But Doing Plenty Destructive

I Guess I Could Go Back
But Desire I Lack

Poem 96

The Night Calls to Me
So Much More to See

The Streets Are Alive
That Is Where I Thrive

So Much Going Down
All Over the Town

So Many People Around
Such A Different Sound

Being Up All Night
Feels So Right

Poem 97

Another Cop Was Shot
That Guy Should Rot

Just Doing Her Job
A Bank They Did Rob

One Bad Guy Dead
Shot Himself in The Head

Time to Mourn the Brave Cop
I Feel Bad for Her Pop

Wish She Was Still Here
Instead of Dead in Her Gear

Poem 98

Once Just an Average Guy
That Is No Lie

Now the Richest Man
Took His Windows and Ran

Went from Nothing
And Became Something

He May Be A Geek
But He Reached the Peak

Poem 99

I Matter How Low I Sank
I Still Always Drank

Had to Drink My Beer
To Hide My Fear

I Was Afraid to Love
Even from Above

Thought There Was No One To Tell
So, I Lived in My Own Hell

Pushed Out My Wife
From My Life

I Lived for My Drink
Life Always on The Brink

What Else Can I Say
I Thought It Was the Only Way

I Guess I Was Wrong
But I Took to Long

Poem 100

You're So Fine
On Your Looks I Dine

Such A Beautiful Girl
My Mind Began to Swirl

You Got Me Hooked
On How You Looked

You Are My Perfect Match
On to You I Latch

With You I Can Achieve Any Goal
Because You Make Me Whole

You Support Me in Everything I Do
I Am What I Am Because Of You

You Comfort Me
Can't You See

You Completed My Life
When You Became My Wife

Poem 101

Feeling So Fucking Fine
Cause on X I Do Dine

Mind Is Racing So Fast
It's Such A Blast

I Can't Believe the Feeling
Oh, So Appealing

Let It Take Its Toll
God, I Love to Roll

Poem 102

God Is All That You Need
Your Soul He Will Feed

Make Your Life Better
Save You from Satan's Shredder

Put Your Trust in The Lord
Protect You from The Evil Horde

Spread His Word of Love
Feel the Grace from Above

He Will Make Sure You Don't Fall
He Is the Creator of It All

His Love Has No End
Jesus, He Did Send

He Should Always Be in Your Mind
Worship Him and Peace You Will Find

When Life Is Tough
If It Gets to Rough

He Will Always Carry You
No Matter What You Do

He Hears All You Say
Each Day

Listen to His Words of Hope
Don't Be A Dope

Shutting Him Out
Because Of Doubt

Is Not A Smart Thing?
Listen to The Angels Sing

Look Him in The Face
And Absorb His Grace

Read from His Book
It Won't Hurt to Look

Poem 103

I Strum My Guitar
At the Local Bar

Make A Buck or Two
Playing Something New

I Have A Good Sound
Hope It Gets Around

Looking for A Break
My Own Music I Make

I Love to Play
My Own Way

Music Sets Me Free
It Means Everything to Me

Poem 104

Up All Night
Ready to Fight

Searching for Trouble
Drinking Another Double

Rage Building Inside
Feeding My Dark Side

Hearing the Train
I Numb the Pain

Poem 105

Should I Go Out on A Limb
And Believe Him

He's Says He Is Being Framed
He Doesn't Want to Be Shamed

Trying to Keep His Good Name
Trying to Preserve His Fame

Needing to Get Clear
To Get Rid of The Fear

Of Going to Jail
Him They Are Trying to Nail

For A Murder of a Priest
On Him the Media Does Feast

I Think He Needs Me
To Keep Him Free

For Him to Avoid the Death Dance
I Am His Best Chance

His Rep Will Always Me Smeared
But I Will Get Him Cleared

Need to Find the Real Killer
Or They'll Hang Him from A Pillar

Errors I Can Afford None
Or I Won't Get the Job Done

I Hope We Have Enough to Win
This Wasn't His Sin

We Are Running Out of Time
To Clear Him of The Crime

I Need to Win This Case
Hope I Can Keep the Pace

Their Case Isn't That Strong
I Think They Have It Wrong

Poem 106

You Don't See Me
So Let Me Be

Tired of Being A Toy
For A Stupid Boy

All You Want to Do Is Fuck
Well You're Out of Luck

Poem 107

I Open Up to The Poor
So, I Can Give More

If They Don’t Pout
I Will Help Them Out

Sometimes I Serve Them Food
When I’m In Mood

Lending A Helping Hand
Can Get Them Out of Quicksand

Hoping They Can Get on Their Feet
Is A Goal I Aim to Meet

Some of The People I Met
Needed Money to Pay A Debt

Sometimes It Is for Power
Or So They Can Take A Shower

A Lot of Them Seemed Sad
Because Of The Life They Had

Now They Show Signs of Hope
Because I Help Them Cope

Their Life Getting Good
As They Prayed It Would

By Trying To Stop Their Strife
I Play A Part in Their Life

When I Go That Extra Mile
It Makes Me Smile

For Them I Fight
For What Is Right

Poem 108

I Have A Vision
Of People in Prison

Serving Out Their Time
Because Of Their Crime

My Vision Is Wrong
They're Not into Long

Sentenced to Fifteen
But Space Is So Lean

So, They're Out in Far Less
It's Such A Mess

Don't Let the System Fail
Keep Them in Jail

Poem 109

I Love to Get High
Give Anything A Try

It A Great Feeling
Floating to The Ceiling

The Drugs I Do Love
Flying Live A Dove

It Make Me Feel So Free
With Drugs Life I Can Flee

Just A Little Trip Away
You Could Say

What A Kick Ass Ride
Let's Out My Other Side

It Keeps Me Sane
To Escape My Pain

Poem 110

Do You Think He Is Real?
What Do You Really Feel

Could He Be Up There
Believe If You Dare

Does He Give Us Hope?
Some Say Nope

I Really Don't Know
But Some Say So

They Seem So Sure
Feeling Beginning to Stir

What If It's All True
What Should I Do

I Think He Might Be Alive
To Help Me Survive

Should I Let His Grace
Set My Pace

I Shouldn't Turn My Back
Cause Salvation I Will Lack

Hope He Guides Me Right
And Shows Me the Light

Poem 111

I Can Recover Any Drive
Make the Data Survive

I Have Special Gift
Threw the Hex A Can Sift

I Can Search Threw the Biggest Pile
To Find Your Missing File

You Data I Will Save
Out from Its Grave

Finding Lost Mail
I Almost Never Fail

Everything Will Be Fine
When I Get You Back Online?

Put Your Trust in Me
And Your Data You Will See

Poem 112

I Tried A DNA
Not Bad I Must Say

It's Kind of a Fruity Drink
I Do Think

It Tastes Kind of Good
Drink More I Should

I Guzzle All I Can
I Am A Drinking Man

I Love to Get Drunk
Gets Me in A Funk

Nowhere to Be Found
I Love to Roam Around

Looking for People to Meet
Walking Down the Street

Alcohol Is A Friend of Mine
Helps Make Me Shine

Brings Out A Side of Me
To Sometimes See

People for What They Are
Even from Afar

Poem 113

Hoping Someday to Be A Star
For Now, I Play at A Bar

It Won't Take Long
To Write My Song

Hopefully It's A Hit
Finally, I Will Fit

Not Just Another Face
Lost in This Place

It Would Be So Fine
If Fame Could Be Mine

I Want People to Know Me
Have My Music Set Them Free

Hope They Enjoy My Sound
Hope It Gets Around

Poem 114

I Sit Back in My Chair
To the Sky I Stare

Gazing Upwards to The Stars
Back Home from The Bars

I'm All Alone
Just Kicking It on My Own

I Have No One In My Life
To Cause Me Any Strife

I Like Having No Ties
Not Hearing Any Lies

I Don't Need Anyone but Me
You Will See

I Need No One To Talk To
With Myself I Make Do

With No One To Fight
I Am Always in The Right

Poem 115

He's Getting Out of The Pen
After Doing Just Ten

Even Thou Get Gutted My Girly
He Still Got Out Early

My Vengeance Will Be Swift
It'll Give My Soul A Lift

He Past Die for His Sin
I Will Surely Grin

To See Him Dead
Will Clear My Head

He Will Feel My Wrath
It Is My Only Path

Now He Must Pay
There Is No Other Way

I Have to Take Him Down
To Take Away My Frown

I Have Waited A long Time
Since He Committed His Crime

I Will Even the Score
And He Will Hurt No More

The Time Is at Hand
To Make My Stand

So, I Can Remain Sane
I Must Cause Him Pain

That Final Blow
Will Kill My Foe

I Need to Be Quick
And Kill This Dick

Then I Can Start to Thrive
That Is for What I Strive

Once He Is the Ground
My Mind Will Be Sound

It Is My Dream
To Make Him Scream

I Want to See His Eyes
As He Slowly Dies

His Death Is for The Best
To Help Protect the Rest

She Was So Dear
That's Why It's Clear

That He Must Die
He Will Know Why

I Am Doing Him In
Why I Must Win

He Cannot Continue Live
He Has Nothing to Give

His Life I Will Take
Dumb His Body in A Lake

I Will Do the Deed
And Let the Gators Feed

Nothing for The Cops to Find
Saves Me from A Possible Bind

I Hate to Break the Law
But What He Did I Saw

I Hope God Will Forgive Me
And Not Punish Thee

I Have to Do It
In His House I Sit

I Wait for Him to Come Back
Must Stay on Track

He Open the Door
I Throw Him to The Floor

Hit Him with A Bat
Got to Kill This Rat

I Hear His Bones Break
Justice I Now Make

Blood Beginning to Flow
Pain His Face Does Show

I Swing with All My Might
It Feels So Right

I Beat Him for So Long
I May Be Wrong

But He Needs to Die This Day
I Must Say

I Am Still Hitting Him
Breaking Every Limb

Broken Bones Everywhere
From the Bat I Share

His Body Goes Still
I Have Had My Fill

I Did What Needed to Be Done
For Him Killing My Hun

He Took His Last Breath
And I Enjoyed His Death

As My Heart Slows from Its Race
I Wipe His Blood from My Face

My Hands Are Still Steady
Because I Was Ready

Poem 116

We Couldn't Get into Oz Fest
We Did Our Best

We Couldn't Get Past the Gate
The Cops We Did Hate

They Found Bill's
Illegal Pills

Because Of Our Sin
They Denied Letting Us In

Poem 117

I Trust in The Almighty Bowl
My Pipe Is My Soul

I Worship Only Pot
Fuck the Red Dot

With It I'll Never Be A Dud
My Savoir Is My Green Bud

I Can Walk on Water or Glass
If I Have My Grass

I See the Angels Dance
Caught in A Hash Filled Trance

Poem 118

I Realize Now He Is There
His Love He Will Share

He Will Always Forgive
For as Long as I Live

No Need to Chase
His Wondrous Grace

He Will Show Me the Way
No Dues to Pay

I Feel the Power of His Light
For My Soul He Does Fight

Poem 119

I See Them Walking Around
Without A Sound

They Are Hard to See
Just Let Them Be

They Float in The Air
Without A Care

No Signs of Life They Show
Threw Walls They Can Go

True Death They Can't Obtain
Trapped in An Ethereal Plane

Poem 120

Did You See Her Go By?
Damn She Was Fly

She Made My Heart Skip A Beat
That's No Easy Feat

I Want Her So Bad
It's Kind of Sad

She Is So Fine
Wish She Was Mine

Poem 121

Stop and Think
About That Drink

You've Gone So Long
It Is Wrong

Put Down the Booze
You Will Lose

From Just One Sip
You Will Slip

Don't Get Lit
You Don't Need It

Poem 122

I Am on A Quest
To Do My Best

Hoping Not to Die
You Know Why

My Level at Stake
In My Armor I Quake

I Feel
I Need A Heal

My Cleric Just Sits
As the Monster Hits

One Bubble to Go
For Me and My Foe

Hope He Starts to Run
Then He'll Be Done

The Wizard Needs to Blast
Kill This Beast at Last

Poem 123

Mushrooms I Can Grow
They Create A Psychedelic Show

So, Drink the Tea
And You Will See

What A Great Feeling
Floating to The Ceiling

Feel Them Starting to Hit
I Am Now So Lit

Things Starting to Appear
I Have No Fear

Poem 124

Life Is a Trial
But I Can Always Smile

No Matter How Beaten I Get
I am Nobody's Pet

The Light Shows My True Side
But I Still Have My Pride

I Will Not Bend
But Soon It May End

Poem 125

See How I Run
It's Not for Fun

I Am Fleeing for My Life
Caused So Much Strife

Caused So Much Pain
For So Little Gain

I Rob and Steal
But Not for a Meal

Just Trying to Get By
Just Trying to Stay High

Poem 126

I Hear the Voices in My Head
From People Long Dead

I Believe They Are from The Past
But How Long Can It Last

Voices of When I Was Young
Now on the Bottom Rung

I Inch Closer to the Ground
But Once was Found

Now I Am in the Dark
Outlook is Stark

Wish I Could Go Back
The Deck to Restack

Innocence Lost Forever
Return It Will Never

Poem 127

I Feel the Pain So Strong
Something Must Be Wrong

My Breath is Low
Heart Rate Slow

Vison Starting to Fold
Feel So Cold

Fighting to Stay Awake
Body Starting to Quake

Like a Tire in a Gutter
I Feel a Shutter

Sound is Cutting Out
There is No Doubt

I Feel the Influx of Fear
As I Think the End is Near

I've Rounded the Bend
And Soon It Will End

Poem 128

I Hear the Train
Even Over the Rain

Family Coming Soon
No More Saloon

It Might Be Dirty Here
But Plenty to Cheer

I Was Bold
And Got My Gold

Living Out West
I Rose to My Best

Cheek Filled with Dip
A Gun on My Hip

Poem 129

I Grab for My Gun
He Begins to Run

He Won't Get Away
He Must Pay

Danger Will Be More
As He Enters a Store

People Start to Yell
I Hear an Alarm Bell

People Getting Down
Scared of This Clown

Behind the Discount Rack
He Runs Out the Back

Have to Take Him Out
Head off His Route

I Am on His Heel
Justice He Will Feel

Poem 130

Seeing the Storm
Starting to Form

Beginning to Live
Starting TO Give

Getting Hit
Because You Don't Fit

Getting Stabbed
Because You Blabbed

Blood Beginning to Flow
Dying Slow

Give It A Chance
With Your Last Dying Glance

Your Heart Begins to Pound
As the World Goes Around

Shot in The Dark
Because You Were A NARC

Poem 131

Lincoln Logs
And Puppy Dogs

Spin the Top
Kill A Cop

It was Your Choice
Listen to The Voice

It Was Your Wish
Your Life Shatters Like A Dish

Your Sentenced to Death
Your Last Dying Breath

Poem 132

Got to Chill
Take A Pill

She's Not Your Type
Hit the Pipe

Snort the Line
You'll Be Just Fine

Hit the Bar
You'll Go Real Far

Grab the Knife
Defend Your Life

Kill Them Dead
Sight Turns Red

Poem 133

I Sit in My Chair
Life Not So Fair

I Sit Here and Drink
Life Continues to Sink

Bottles All Around
Spilling on the Ground

Wish She Was Still Here
But I Still Have My Beer

Poem 134

Life Is Not What You Thought
Happiness Can't Be Bought

Destined to Be More
But Really Life Is Poor

Want to End Your Life
Cut Yourself with A Knife

Pain Is All You Feel
No Way to Heal

Hope to Take A Last Breath
Because You Pray for Death

Poem 135

Too Much Pain
Listen to The Rain

Saddens the Heart
To Be Apart

You Left Me Hear
I Have So Much Fear

Going on Without You
There Are So Few

People That You Can Love
Your Soul Like A Dove

Raises Up High
Towards the Sky

Poem 136

Everyone Knows Your Name
You Have Hit Ultimate Fame

You're a Household Word
By the Things They Have Heard

Arrested for Drugs
You Just Shrug

Seen with A Whore
Cool to The Core

Teens Worship You
You've Had A Few

Parents Protest
Because You're Grotesque

Not A Role Model
Parents Love to Coddle

Their Babies from Life
To Protect Them from Strife

Let the Kids Be
Let Them Free

Your Grasp Will Kill
The Youths Strong Will

Poem 137

The Whistle Blows
The Hatred Grows

You Get in Your Car
And Go to A Bar

You Go to Her House
Rip Open Her Blouse

Watch Her Frown
Slice Her Down

Here Her Scream
While You Cream

Poem 138

Shoot It In
Begin to Grin

Feel It Race
Back to Your Pace

Mind Begins to Float
Sailing on A Boat

Feel the Wind in Your Hair
Feeling That Is So Rare

You Want It Some More
You're Such A Whore

Sell Your Cock
Go into Hock

Steal If You Must
For What You Lust

Heroin Is Your Friend
Till the Bitter End

Poem 139

Driving to Work
In the Shadows He Lurks

Waiting for My Time
Dropping the Dime

My Life Soon Will End
Just Around the Bend

Accident Coming Soon
Dead by Noon

Hit by A Car
Hospital to Far

Dead Behind the Wheel
Death Is Now Real

Poem 140

The Start of The War
What's One More

Killing for Some Cause
Without A Pause

We Send Out Our Boys
They're A Politicians Toys

Killed in The Night
Bodies Lost in A Fight

Battle Rages On
Governments Con

Telling Us Lies
To Strengthen Ties

Politics Feeding the Press
What A Mess

Planes Overhead
Lives They Shred

Bombs Falling Fast
People Killed by The Blast

They're Not to Blame
Caught in The Game

Poem 141

Get on The Plane
In the Pouring Rain

It Leaves the Ground
New York Bound

Look at The Lightning
Quite Frightening

Thunder Rattles
The Storm Battles

Lightning Hits
The Plane Splits

It Begins to Start
To Break Apart

Heading for The Ocean
I Think You Get the Notion

Poem 142

I Place My Bet
And Light My Cigarette

I Look at My Cards and Think
As I Take A Sip from My Drink

Need This Hand to Come In
I Really Need This Win

Need Just One More
To Make A Score

My Hand Looks Good
I Hoped It Would

I Know It's A Good Hand
Money I Should Land

Everything Will Be Fine
If This Pot Is Mine

I Lay My Cards Down
Faces Begin to Frown

I Win the Pot
Damn I'm Hot

Poem 143

Smoke Your Hash
Feel the Crash

See It Flip
Flesh Begins to Rip

Skids on Its Side
Oh, What A Ride

See Them Bleed
Life They Now Need

Help Is Sure to Arrive
Not That You're Alive

Haiku

1

Snort A Line of Coke
Feeling Numbness In My Nose
I Feel The Rush Hit

2

Body Is Shaking
I'm Tilting The Bottle Back
Calm Begins To Take

3

Feeling That Rush Now
Flying Higher Than Before
Crashing Back To Soon

4

I Embrace My Sin
Heart And Soul Are Void Of Light
God, Forsaken Me

5

My Death Approaches
The Straps Firmly Tightened Down
Injections Begins

6

Shot Down Like A Dog
Have Been Hunted For So Long
Unable To Flee

7

Locked Within A Cell
Forced To Live In A Prison
Body, Heart, Mind, and Soul

8

His Almighty Grace
Light Illuminating All
Clearing Out Darkness

9

I Must Be Insane
Cannot Stop All The Voices
Always There Waiting

10

The Gun In My Mouth
The Tears Drip Off Of My Face
I Pull The Trigger

11

Waiting For The Start
Tonight, The Engines Rev High
Clutch Drops, The Car Goes

12

Freedom, A Mindset
Prison, A Reality
Death, A Welcome Fate

13

Try To Tap The Vein
Have To Chase That High Again
I Want It… Need It

14

Stabbed Hard In The Chest
Ripping Through Tormented Soul
Relieving Life's Pain

15

Picking At My Skin
Haven't Slept So Many Days
My Body Rotting

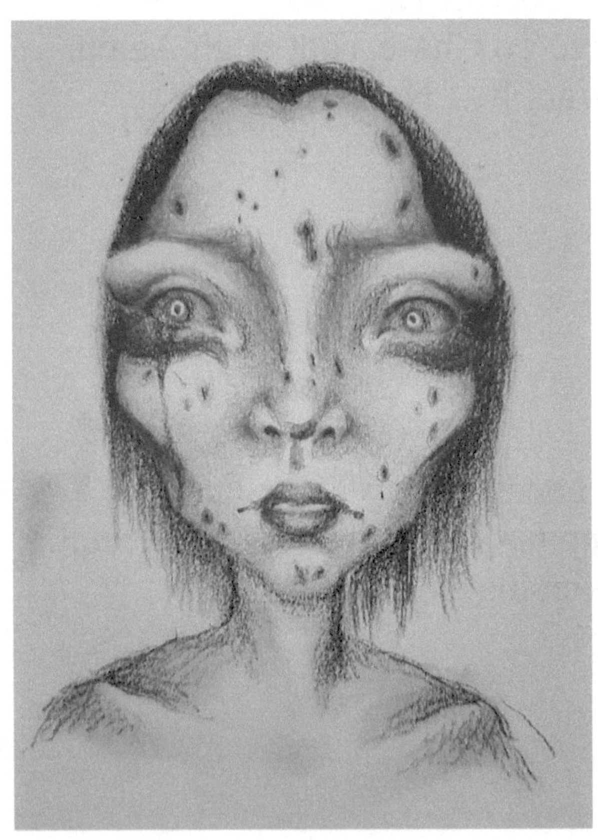

16

Feeling Fucking Free
Just Falling, Soaring, Flying
Ground Rushing Up Fast

17

Wondering Around
Their Souls Trapped In A Shell
The Living Dead Walk

18

Drinking My Cold Beer
Washing Away My Deep Fear
My Eyes Do So Tear

19

Snort The White Powder
My Nose Always Goes So Numb
I Now Own The World

20

I Feel So Sickened
Cold Sweat Drips Down My Forehead
Where Is My Dealer

21

Trapped In My Dark Cell
Imprisoned In My Own Mind
The Screams Never Stop

22

Laying In The Street
Blood Spilling From My Split Head
Left To Die Again

23

I Feel Satan’s Grip
Entered My Soul On A Trip
Will Never Let Go

24

Wondering Around
Homeless Living On The Street
The Wondering Dead

25

Falling Through The Cracks
Struggling Just To Live My Life
Lost In The System

26

Misery Of Life
Piercing My Soul To The Core
Beaten Down By Life

27

Clean And Free At Last
Sobriety Is My Air
I Can Breathe Again

28

A Sweet Kid He Was
He Snapped Like An Animal
Put Down Like A Dog

29

Parents Dead So Long
Became A Loner In Life
Hiding From The World

30

Caught In Your Own Lies
Living The Lies In Your Head
Wondering And Lost

31

Falling From The Sky
Wind Rustling By Very Fast
Soaring Like A Bird

32

Gods Loving Light Shines
Shown Down On So Many Souls
But It's Lost On Me

33

Needle Stuck In Arm
Drugs Flowing Freely Through Me
My Life Is My Death

34

Stuck Out In The Woods
My Mind Is Like A Forrest
Trees Fall Silently

35

Like Being Alone
Far From All Other People
Just Living For Me

36

Helping People Live
Saving Their Eternal Soul
Gods Servants To Man

37

Deep Within My Head
I Know I Fuel Hatred
Poison In My Veins

38

Hide Under The Bed
Saw The Splattering of Red
They Are Surely Dead

39

I Hear The Siren
Blackness Entering Vision
Will They Be In Time

40

My Father Of Mine
So Much More To Give Us All
Died Too Soon In Life

41

Seeing A Future
Remembering All The Past
Celebrating Life

42

Trapped In A Dark Mine
Engulfed In Total Darkness
Struggling To Just Breathe

43

I Hear The Motors
Running Of The World Machine
Stop Them If I Could

44

Send Boys To Slaughter
Creating War Among Men
The Leaders Of Man

45

Now Missing My Legs
Lost In A Fight For Freedom
Doing The Right Thing

46

Returning From War
Adjusting To My New Life
Patient Is My Wife

47

Lost In Deep Dark Thought
Now Searching For Something More
Not Sure What To Do

48

Drugs On The Corner
Someone Is Going To Gain
Money Over Life

49

True In My Own Mind
Singing A Different Tune
It Will Change This Time

50

Domestic Terror
Drugs Flowing Like A River
Shattering Our Youth

51

Skipping Rocks All Day
Lost In My Young Childhood Youth
Not Knowing The World

52

Playing With Others
Difficult To Get Along
Children Filled With Hate

53

Dying Like Embers
Taken Over By The Drugs
Dealers Peddle Them

54

Seeing Clouds Above
The Soaring Of A White Dove
Gods Eternal Love

55

I Am Who I Am
I'm Not A Religious Man
I Give My Own Peace

56

Not Looking To Die
But It Will Come For Us All
I Do Not Feel Fear

57

Tears Run From Her Eye
Looking At Her Dead Husband
Sorrow In Her Heart

58

Like Little Lost Sheep
They Are Slaughtered In Their Sleep
Pain Running So Deep

59

Traded My Own Soul
For Riches, Bitches, And Fame
A Hollywood Life

60

Crazy As A Fox
My Own Lies Always Be True
President Am I

61

Dumbass Liberals
Not Seeing The Real World
Living Delusion

62

Right Against The Left
Neither Will Bend Anymore
The Real Problem

63

Never Seen Again
Live On In Our Memory
Are The Good Old Days

64

Our Sad Broken World
Violence On All Levels
Nothing New To Us

65

Smoker, A Toker
Burning Well Past My Midnight
I'm Living My Life

66

I'm Out In The Black
Free To My Own Way Of Life
To Me Flying Free

67

You Always Tell Me
How Am I Suppose To Feel
But I'm Not Able

68

The Big Tree Falls Down
Hear It Crash To The Hard Ground
But I Am Alone

69

If The Water Leaks
And The Candle Light Is Fire
Maybe All Is Lost

70

Randomness of Death
Can Strike Out All Of Mankind
Where Is Your Soul Now

71

Thoughtless People Live
Living Amongst All Of Us
Using Up Our Air

72

Danger In Our Air
Toxic And Deadly Terror
The Weapons Of Death

73

A Shortness of Breath
Shooting Pain Starts Down Your Arm
The Reaper Watches

74

My Body Is Trapped
My Mind Is My Own Temple
I Am Free To Think

75

At Its Beck And Call
Still Chained Like An Animal
I Can’t Put It Down

76

I Feel The Power
It's Cold But Embraces Me
My One Friend, My Gun

77

Beer Is So Tasty
I Like Beer And It Likes Me
Beer Is My Best Friend

78

I Lay Here In Bed
Facing The Reaper Of Death
He Now Laughs At Me

79

Caught In The Middle
A Child Used As A Weapon
No One Cares For Them

80

The Picture Doesn't Show
The Dread In My Eyes And Soul
Beaten Night And Day

81

Two Men Still Fighting
Both Refusing To Give In
Will We Always Watch

82

I Hear The Angels
In The Laughter Of Children
It Always Fades Out

83

Passion Of The Youth
Builds Worlds And Can Move
Mountains
The Old Bring Despair

84

Life Evolves With Us
A Bitterness Breeds With Age
Death Becomes Freedom

85

With Age Comes Wisdom
With Wisdom Comes Ones Purpose
With Purpose Comes Life

86

Not About Nature
But It Is Still A Haiku
Fucking Deal With It

87

A Ship Lost At Sea
Waves Crashing Over The Bow
Death Awaits For Them

88

Plane Is Going Down
People Praying In Their Seats
Too Little To Late

89

I Open My Chute
Falling Down Into The DMZ
Entering Combat

90

Waiting By The Phone
Wondering If She'll Call Back
Silence Is Endless

91

Watching For The Light
Lost In My Hidden Dark Place
Smothering Darkness

92

Filled With Rage And Hate
Joy Of Pain And Suffering
Causing Wounds To Man

93

Eyes Bleary And Red
The Crown is Heavy And Worn
Victory Is Near

94

Bound By A Blood Oath
Sworn To Die And To Protect
Saving The Princess

95

Plague Begins To Spread
Across The Air And The Sea
Ending The Known World

96

Waves Crash On The Shore
Wind Gusts Across The Ocean
Clouds Turn Dark And Gray

97

Strapped On A Table
Sentence Being Carried Out
My Death Is Coming

98

The Clock Stares At Me
It's Ticking Down Till The End
Life Ebbing Away

99

Lost In The Desert
Searching For Water, For Food
Sun Draining My Life

100

Running Wild Tonight
I'm Higher Than I Should Be
Loving This Moment

101

Traded In My Soul
Living The Corporate World
Money Is My God

102

Life Feeling Empty
Since She Was Taken Away
Trying To Find Peace

103

War Of All Nations
Over Religious Dogma
Peace Is Without God

104

Nations Torn Apart
Disease Ravaging The Poor
Third World Suffering

105

Decided To Go
Grateful For What We Once Had
Must Choose To Go On

106

Hitting The Pipe Hard
Feeling The Train In My Head
Craving My Cocaine

107

Seeing The Blue Skies
Feeling Free As I Take Flight
Soaring Through The Air

108

Living In The Camp
Captured By A Crazy Man
Double Eight Of Hate

109

Grape Of The Mad Dog
Prefer Milk Of The Poppy
But Anything Works

110

Wondering Around
Finding Something To Live For
My Soul Finding Peace

111

My Head Is Pounding
Feels Like I Have Been Beaten
Body Shutting Down

112

Laying In Gutter
Piece Of Trash In The Bayou
Just Like The City

113

Leaves Fluttering Down
The Wind Blows Freely In Gusts
The Sun Shines Brightly

114

The Stars Out Of Reach
Long To Return To The Sky
Stranded, Stuck, Lost, Dead

115

The Funeral Pyre
Burns High In The Dark Night Sky
Valhalla He Goes

116

Set Off From The Shore
Look To Pillage And Plunder
Ah The Pirates Life

117

Sweat Lining My Brow
Dilated And Blurry Eyes
Just Living The Life

118

Heart Beating, Racing
Adrenaline Speeding Through
The Rush Of Power

119

Poor Mother Nature
Feeling The Pain Of The World
Living The Slow Death

120

Laying In A Bath
Red Starts Filling The Water
Life Ebbing Away

121

Looking At People
I Think It's Kind Of Funny
How Dumb They Can Be

122

Is Full Of Self Doubt
Every Time He Sees Himself
Unsure Of His Life

123

Lost In Emotion
Has Forgotten Who He Was
Grief Stricken His Heart

124

Living My Life Clean
I Found My Serenity
Seeing Things Clearly

125

Killer Of Giants
Metal Mountains Of Madness
Still Flexing Their Might

126

The End Is Coming
For My Heart, Mind, And My Soul
I Embrace What Comes

127

Flying Like A Dove
Soaring Through The Open Sky
Peace, Serenity

128

Innocence Is Lost
Buried In A Shallow Grave
Her Dead Body Found

129

My Dealer Helps Me
He Waits On The Street Corner
Knowing I'll Be Back

130

He Was So Not Pleased
I Couldn't Stop Laughing At Him
I Am Still John Doe

131

Darkness Surrounds Me
Enveloping Who I Am
Struggling For The Light

132

Living Life's Struggles
What Is Your Emergency
But Just Speak Slowly

133

Walking In The Park
Feeling The Gentle Air Flow
She Completes My Life

134

My Future Is Bleak
A Shotgun Pressed To My Cheek
I Cause My Own Death

135

I Sit In My Chair
I See Her Fear And Her Tears
They Put On My Hood

136

Hit The Crystal Shard
Begins To Smoke As I Toke
I’m Soaring So High

137

For All Of Her Lies
Feeling Her Life Ebb Away
Her Life She Now Lacks

Thank You
11/14/11

Brett C. Persson
brettpersson@gmail.com

Other Works By:

S.C. Persson

www.scpersson.art

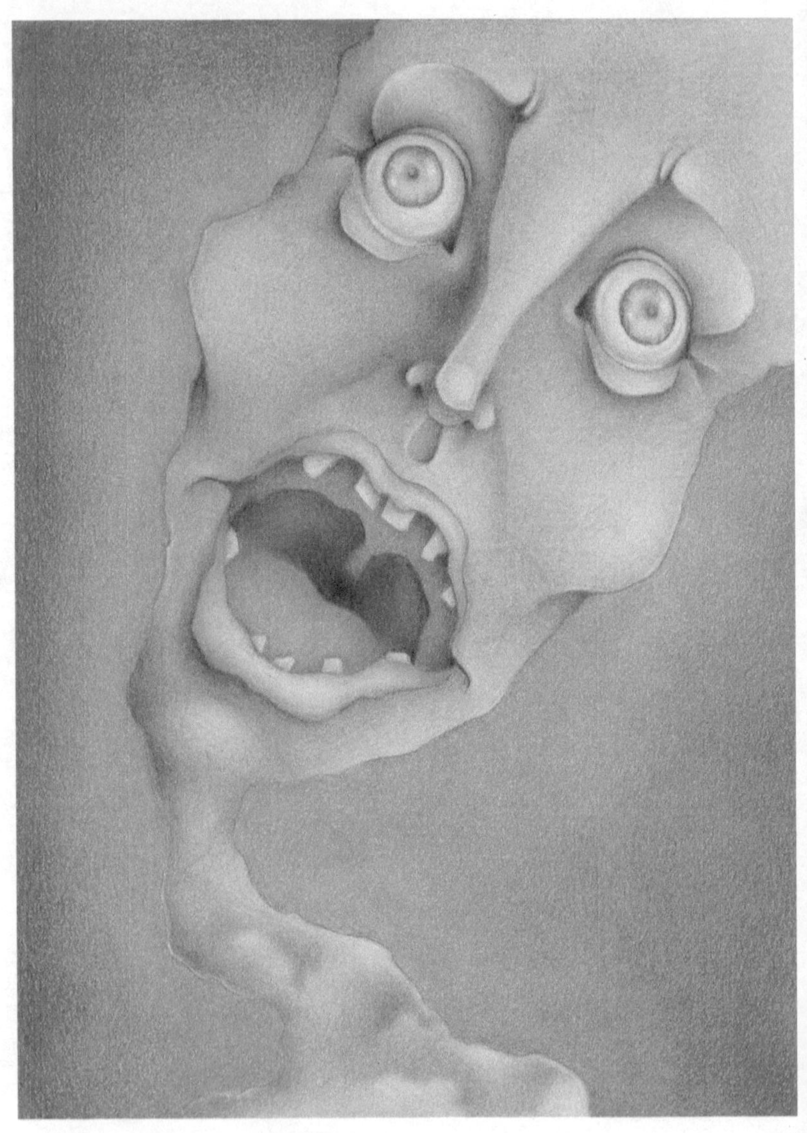

/

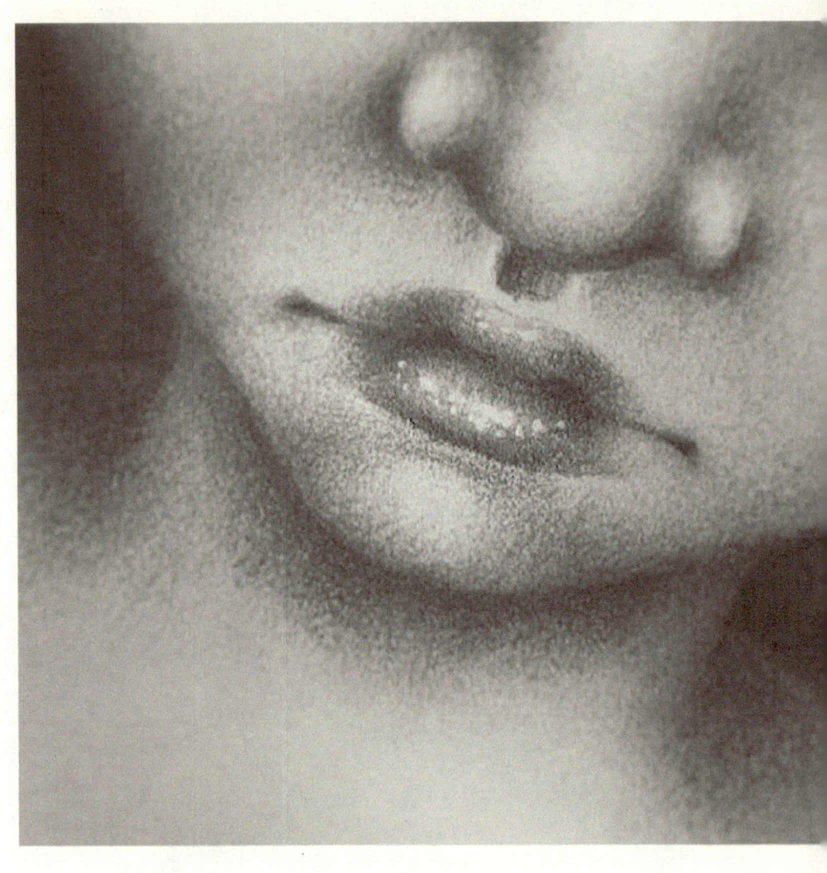

www.ingramcontent.com/pod-product-compliance
Lightning Source LLC
LaVergne TN
LVHW091037080826
845145LV00002B/525

* 9 7 8 1 9 6 4 7 9 3 9 1 7 *